Red Roger

*Happy Birthday
TOMIKO!
—i hope you have fun
being 4!
love,
Jules (91)*

BELLEW PUBLISHING: LONDON

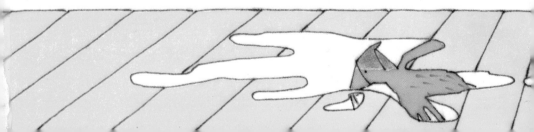

For
Baxbakualanuxsiwae
and all his friends.

First published in Great Britain in 1988 by
Bellew Publishing Company Limited
7 Southampton Place, London WC1A 2DR

ISBN 0 947792 08 2

Printed and bound in Spain by Graficas Estella, S.A.

Red Roger,
the most feared pirate captain
on the high seas,
ruled his ship with terrible ferocity.

He was a bad loser
and, in his rages, spared
neither man…

…nor beast: the ship's cat
suffered dreadfully from his
cruel jests.

Roger's only tender feelings were
reserved for his pet crocodile.

One morning, he yelled down from
the poop deck ordering his favourite
food: 'Spaghetti alla Bolognese, ye scum,
and step on it!'

Immediately, the cook got to work, heating
olive oil in a thick-bottomed iron pan and chopping
the ingredients into tiny slivers.

Then, to his dismay, he found there were no onions
in the veg. rack.

…not even a shallot.

Knowing he must tell his captain
of his failure, he tremblingly mounted the
companionway, pausing only to clip the
kitchen boy's ear.

'You blinking idiot!'
shouted Roger.'We'll have to go and rob
some now.'

After hours of searching, they
overhauled a small vegetable trader
and forced him to give up
all his onions.

Very soon, the cook had prepared
an excellent Spaghetti alla
Bolognese. It was examined critically.

Roger ate noisily.

Hardly had he finished, when he turned into a parrot.
He pecked himself to see whether he was dreaming.

Unbeknown to the pirates, the small
vegetable trader was a conjurer
and had given them trick onions.

The crocodile,
who hated surprises, made off quickly.

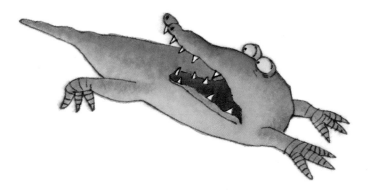

The parrot fluttered up to the bridge and it soon
became clear that he no longer commanded the respect
of his crew.

Rejoicing that their fierce captain had turned into a harmless bird, the crew went their own way, pursuing defenceless merchantmen to ask if they wanted anything.

The pirates were generous and kind to
everyone they met and became
welcome at all the ports they sailed into.
The parrot maintained an angry silence.

But, little by little, the pirates taught
the parrot to speak, making sure
he learned only pleasant things like
'Excuse me' and 'If you please'.

Before long, the parrot became more sociable and kept the pirates company in the evenings. 'Good morning! After you! Bless you!' he squawked.

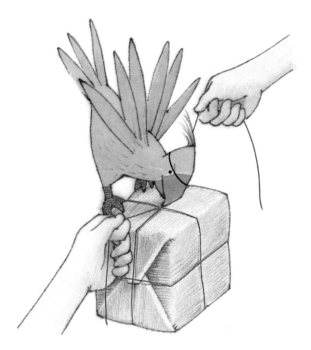

He even found ways to make
himself useful about the ship.

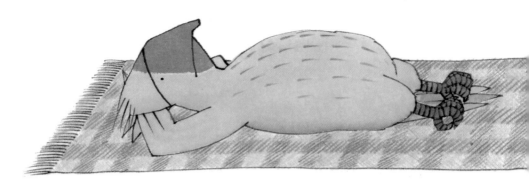

The parrot was lying down one day, thinking of his past life. He began to regret the rotten way he used to make his living when…

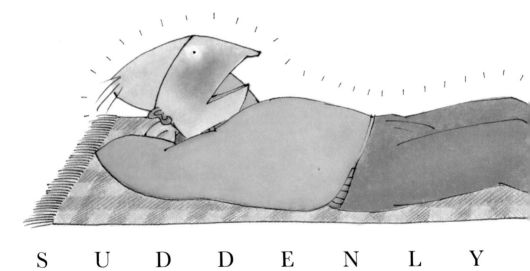

S U D D E N L Y

Trick onions don't work on good people.

This Roger was a new man.
He became famous for
his perfect manners…

…and his faultless habits.

From then on, Roger spent most of his time

sitting in a deck-chair drinking cocoa.

He never behaved like a beast again…

...except sometimes.